Susan E. Snyder

Shivers and Shakes

McCabe Children's Press

ISBN 0-9767163-5-6

To my beautiful
granddaughter Alyssa...
...another joy in my life!
Love,
Grandma

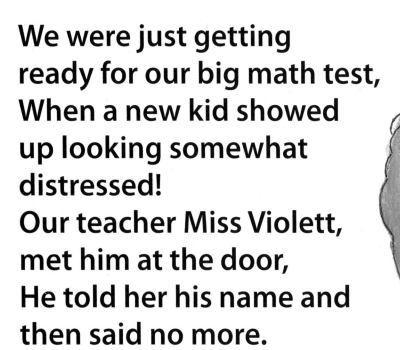

We were just getting
ready for our big math test,
When a new kid showed
up looking somewhat
distressed!
Our teacher Miss Violett,
met him at the door,
He told her his name and
then said no more.

His name was Sam
and it was quite clear,
He wished he was
ANYWHERE other
than HERE!
He had fiery red hair
and bright green eyes,
With a hint of mischief
we could ALL recognize.

He did not talk at all that day.
I guess he didn't have much to say.
But out at recess Sam was pokin' around,
At something green
that was on the ground.

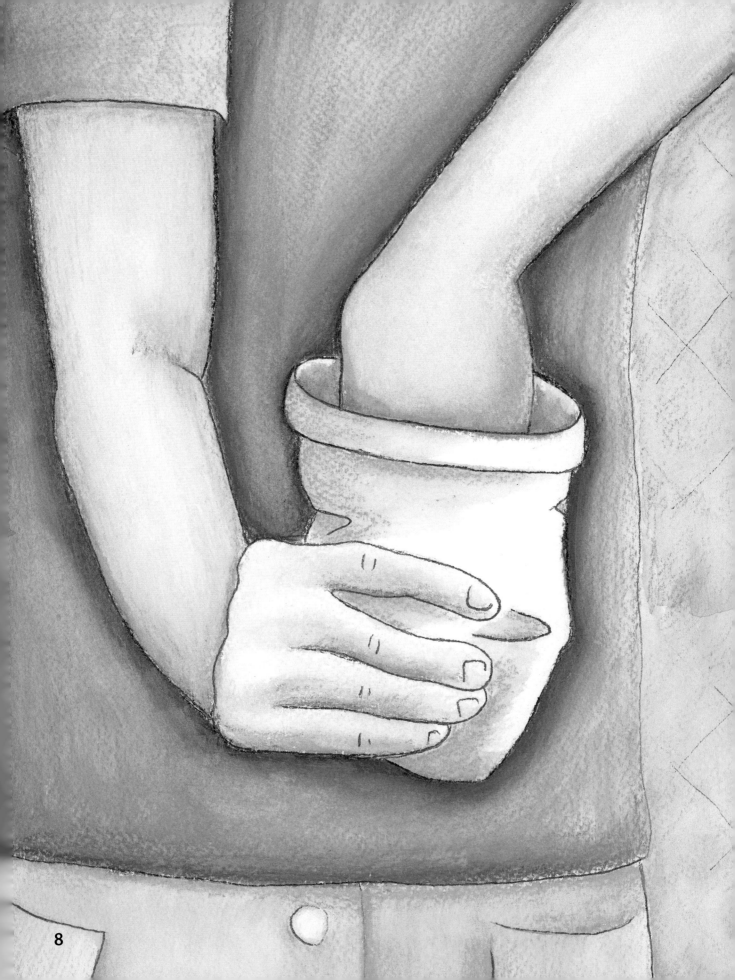

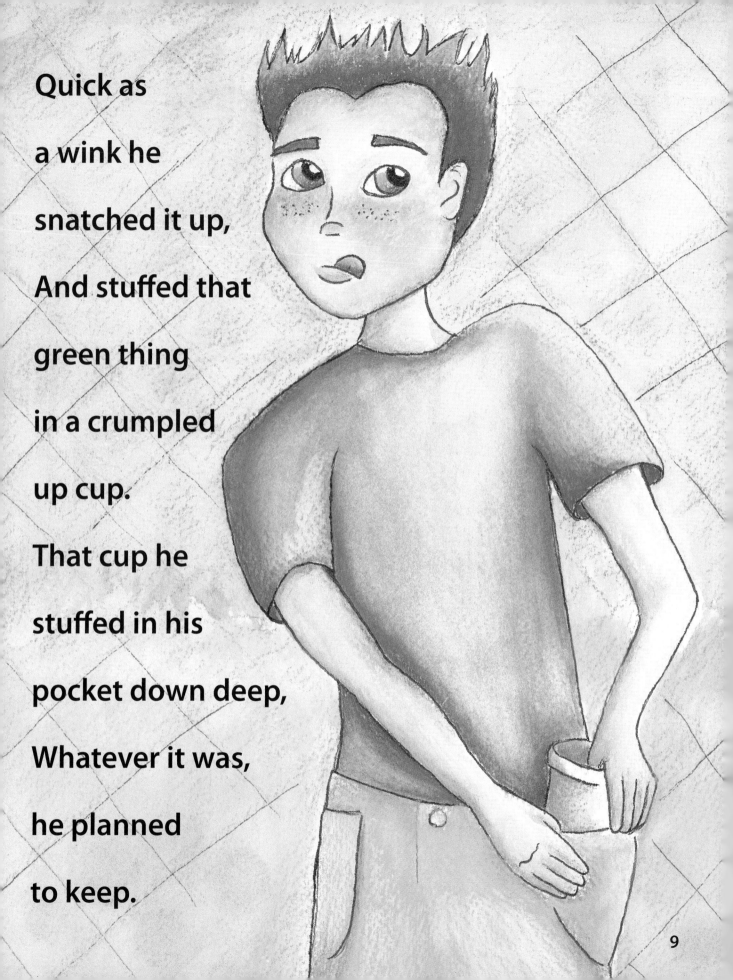

Quick as
a wink he
snatched it up,
And stuffed that
green thing
in a crumpled
up cup.
That cup he
stuffed in his
pocket down deep,
Whatever it was,
he planned
to keep.

9

The very next
day when we got to school,
Sam was first in class, sitting there like "Joe Cool".
There was something sneaky about that guy,
I wasn't sure what and I wasn't sure why.

Suddenly, I heard a sound so shrill, Right down my spine it sent a chill! There was Miss Violett standing up on a chair, Screaming and trying to get away from there! We sat there just staring as she kept climbing up. And now we all knew what Sam stuffed in that cup!

13

There in her desk, peeking out of a drawer,
We saw what Miss Violett was screaming for!
A little green snake just looking around,
Trying to find his way to the ground!

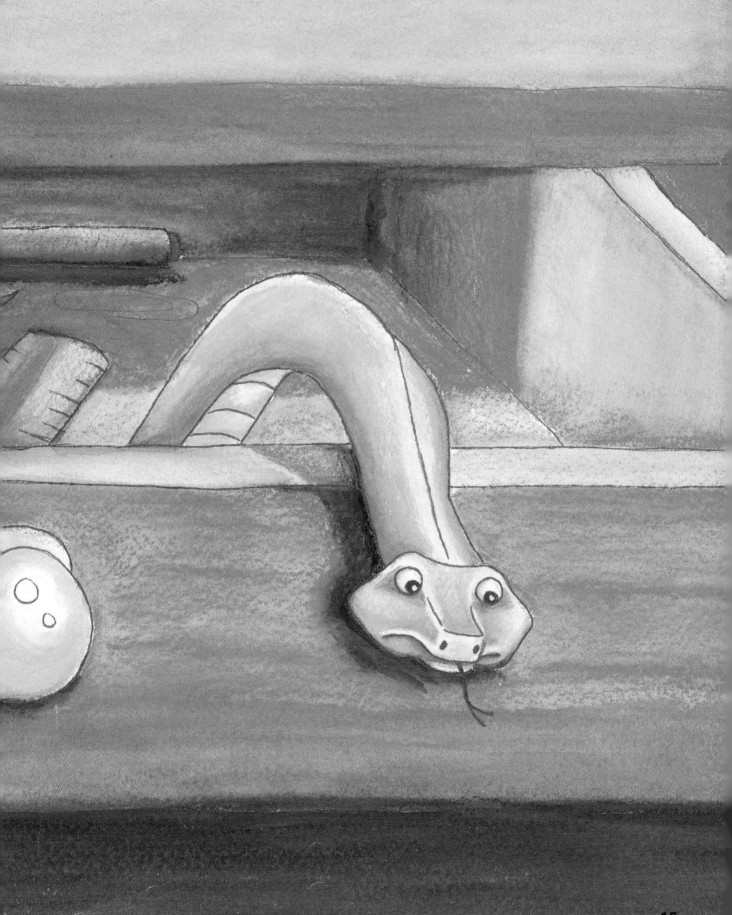

Now, we ALL know Miss Violett is REAL scared of snakes! They give her the SHIVERS; they give her the SHAKES. It does not matter much at all what kind of snake should come to call.

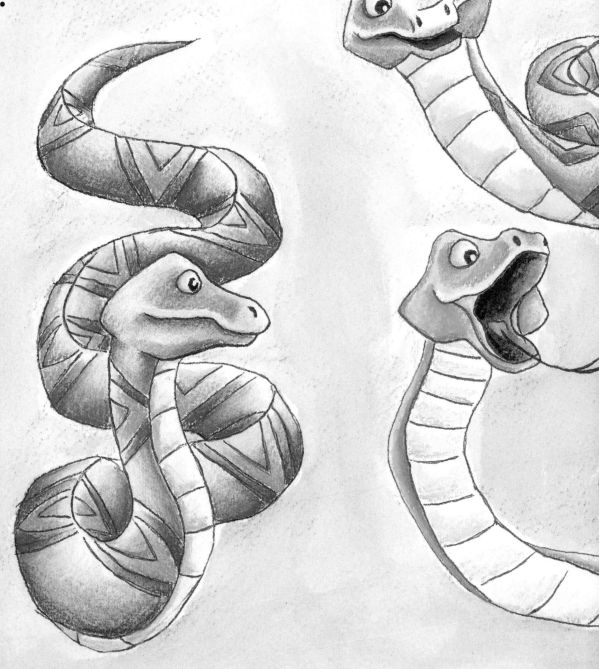

She will yell and scream in total fright if ANY snake comes into sight!

Short, fat snakes,
or long and thin,
Stripes or spots
upon their skin,
It does not
matter HOW
big or small,
ANY snake, she
hates them ALL!
If snakes were
purple with
bright pink
spots, It would
not matter,
she hates
snakes LOTS!
If snakes
were soft
with fluffy fur,
I think that
they would
STILL scare her!

She'd do ANYTHING
to avoid a snake!
Bringing one
to school would be
a HUGE mistake!
So there was Miss
Violett standing up
on a chair in front
of our class,
She did not care!
She climbed from
a chair up onto a desk,
She was screaming and shaking,
WHERE WOULD SHE
GO NEXT?

From the desk to the bookcase, she kept climbing up,
As that little green snake slithered past her tea cup.
Next he slithered across her opened grade book,
While Miss Violett screamed and shivered and shook!
He slithered across Miss Violett's whole desk.
He slithered on homework, her plan book and tests.

We all sat there frozen,
Just watching this scene,
The results of a trick
so sneaky and MEAN!
Then that little green
snake dropped
down to the floor,
And made his escape
through the
opened back door.

25

Miss Violett
climbed down
from the shelves,
desk and chair,

26

Still shivering and shaking, but Sam didn't care.
The next thing we heard was Sam dare to say,
"April Fools' Day, Miss Violett,
gotcha real good today!"

I doubt that sam
knew she was
SO scared of
snakes;
That she'd get
the shivers
and she'd get
the shakes,
That she'd scream
and climb up
on a chair,
Then a desk
and a bookcase
to escape
from there!
Well, needless to
say, Sam soon
met our Dean.
He spent three
days at home
for his prank
so mean.

29

Yes, THAT was a day I remember real well!
A story we ALL still love to tell.
And as for Miss Violett and her fear of snakes,
I think that she STILL has the shivers and shakes!

Needless to say, if you find a snake,
I'm warning you now, don't make Sam's mistake!
I'm not really sure that Sam learned from his trick,
Because today he was poking at the ground with
a stick. And I heard him talking about a fear
of Miss Snyder's,
He was telling
someone, "She's
REAL scared of
SPIDERS!"

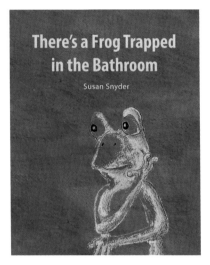

There's a Frog Trapped in the Bathroom
Susan Snyder

The Very Stubborn Centipede
Susan Snyder

More fine books from McCabe Childrens' Press, a division of Kotzig Publishing, Inc.

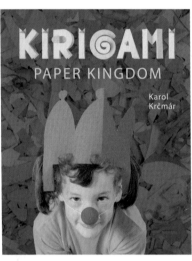

KIRIGAMI
PAPER KINGDOM
Karol Krčmár

KIRIGAMI
GREETING CARDS
Karol Krčmár

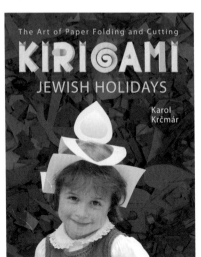

The Art of Paper Folding and Cutting
KIRIGAMI
JEWISH HOLIDAYS
Karol Krčmár

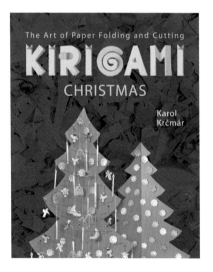

The Art of Paper Folding and Cutting
KIRIGAMI
CHRISTMAS
Karol Krčmár

Susan E. Snyder

Shivers and Shakes

Graphic design and Typography: Radoslav Tokoš
Illustration: Anna Johanson
Editor: Susan McCabe
Published by McCabe Children's Press
A division of Kotzig Publishing, Inc.
Printed in Slovakia
32 pages, 1st edition

www.kotzigpublishing.com

ISBN 0-9767163-5-6